ThunderTrucks! is published by Stone Arch Books
a Capstone imprint
1710 Roe Crest Drive
North Mankato, Minnesota 56003
www.mycapstone.com

Cataloging-in-Publication Data is available on the
Library of Congress website.

ISBN: 978-1-4965-6491-7 (library hardcover)
ISBN: 978-1-4965-6495-5 (eBook)

Summary: Hercules and Theseus are trying to earn
bragging rights of who is the best hero truck of all
time. So they challenge each other to a race through
the Underworld.

Designed by Brann Garvey

Printed in the United States of America
PA021

THUNDERTRUCKS!
UNDERWORLD CLASH

BY BLAKE HOENA
ILLUSTRATED BY FERN CANO

STONE ARCH BOOKS
a capstone imprint

CONTENTS

CHAPTER 1

THUNDERTRUCK XTREME RALLY

Excited trucks fill up the stands. They honk and beep as they cheer on their favorite ThunderTrucks.

An official hooks one end of a chain to Hercules' bumper. She hooks the other end to Theseus' bumper. A mud pit bubbles and belches between the two rivals.

The Tug-o-War Championship

at the ThunderTruck

Xtreme Rally is about

to begin!

"You won't beat me this

time!" Hercules shouts.

"We'll see about that," Theseus

rumbles.

"Competitors, get

ready," the official blares.

The chain between

Hercules and Theseus snaps tight.

TCHING!

"Get set!"

The ThunderTrucks rev their engines.

VROOM! VROOM!

"Pull!"

Tires screech. Dirt
flies. Engines roar.

Theseus jerks forward.
He drags Hercules, tires spinning,
toward the pit.

Mud bubbles up and splashes the
mighty ThunderTruck.

"Eat mud!" Theseus yells.

At the edge of the pit, the treads of
Hercules' tires dig in.

"Not this time," Hercules shouts. His engine rumbles. **RUMBLE! RUMBLE!** He tugs and yanks and jerks. Inch by inch, he drags Theseus toward the pit.

Theseus' tires spin. His engine whines. He kicks up a cloud of dirt. But nothing can stop the mighty Hercules.

Theseus lands in the pit with a SPLASH! Oozing mud covers him from tailpipe to windshield.

"Looks like you need to hit the car wash!" Hercules laughs.

Other ThunderTrucks rush over to congratulate Hercules.

"Wow, I thought Theseus was going win," Atalanta says.

"Great match, Hercules!" Perseus says.

Hercules just puffs out a cloud of exhaust and rolls away. Theseus crawls out of the mud pit and heads in another direction.

* * *

The next competition at the ThunderTruck Xtreme Rally is about to start. Hercules rolls up in front of a ramp. Beyond is a row of flaming tires. He revs his engine. **VROOM!** **VROOM!** Then he takes off in a cloud of dust.

Hercules hits the ramp and leaps into the air. He flies over 10 . . . 20 . . . 30 . . . 40 . . . 47 flaming tires.

The crowd beeps, "Hercules! Hercules!"

As Hercules drives by Theseus, he honks, "Beat that!"

Theseus looks at the flags atop the stadium. They flutter in the wind. Theseus waits until they point away from him. With the wind at his back, he is off. He hits the ramp. He sails over 10 . . . 20 . . . 30 . . . 40 . . . 50 . . . 52 flaming tires.

The crowd beeps, "Theseus! Theseus!"

"Yeah!" he shouts. "I won."

Other ThunderTrucks rush over to congratulate Theseus.

"I didn't think you could beat Hercules' jump," B-phon says.

"That was incredible, Theseus," Argonutz says.

Theseus just puffs out a cloud of exhaust and rolls away. Hercules leaves in another direction. The rest of the ThunderTrucks are confused.

"What is wrong with those two?" Atalanta asks.

"They are getting way too competitive," Odysseus says.

At the next competition, things only get worse. Theseus and Hercules face off at a starting line.

"I am the best ThunderTruck there is!" Theseus roars.

"No, I am the World's Mightiest Truck!" Hercules rumbles. "I even have a decal that says so."

"Anyone can buy one of those at Royal Rumbler's Decal Shop," Theseus backfires.

The other ThunderTrucks drive between the two.

"Stop it!" Perseus says. "You two are supposed to be friends."

No one can believe that the two friends are arguing so much.

"We need a contest to decide who is the best!" Hercules beeps. "Like completing the Rough & Tough Twelve."

"Or racing through the Monster Maze," Theseus honks.

The two ThunderTrucks honk and beep at each other. Then a mysterious MonsterTruck rolls over. It is black with tinted windows. A skull sticks out of the grill.

"You need something more challenging," the truck says in a raspy voice.

"What do you have in mind?" Hercules beeps.

"I challenge you to race through the Underworld," the truck says.

Theseus and Hercules look at each other.

"I'm in!" Hercules rumbles.

"Me too," Theseus blares.

The other ThunderTrucks gasp in shock. Only trucks that cannot be repaired go to the Underworld.

And none of them have ever returned.

CHAPTER 2

THE RIVER STICKY

The next day, Hercules and Theseus meet in front of a large cave. A neon sign above the door flashes the word "Underworld."

A stream of trucks rolls through the gate. They are run-down rust buckets. Some putter along. Others sputter and cough out puffs of smoke. Some are all dented up. Others limp along on broken axles and flat tires. None look repairable.

The black MonsterTruck rolls up to Hercules and Theseus.

"Many enter the Underworld," the MonsterTruck says. "None have returned."

Theseus and Hercules look at each
other.

"That's about to change," Hercules
rumbles.

"Yeah, because I will be the first!"
Theseus shouts.

"Then get ready," the dark truck says.

Theseus and Hercules roll up to the
edge of the cave. Both look determined.

"Get set!"

The two ThunderTrucks rev their
engines. *VROOM! VROOM!*

"Go!"

Tires spin and dirt flies as Hercules and
Theseus take off.

ZOOM! They dart into the cave and enter the Underworld. Inside is a dark and rocky tunnel. It twists and turns as it slopes down into blackness.

Both of the ThunderTrucks flick on their headlights.

They weave in and out of the rust buckets. They speed through the tunnel.

First, Theseus takes the lead. "Ha! I'm winning," he honks.

Then, Hercules darts in front. "I'm gonna win!" he beeps.

Suddenly, the tunnel opens up into a large cavern. Hundreds of beat-up and dented trucks sputter and putter along. They head toward a bridge that crosses a dark, oily river.

Theseus and Hercules try to weave through the other trucks. But there are too many of them. They come screeching to a halt in the world's largest traffic jam. The dark MonsterTruck rolls up to them.

"This is your first
challenge," he says.

"Whoa, you scared
me," Hercules beeps in
surprise.

"Where did you come from?" Theseus
asks.

The MonsterTruck does not answer.
Instead, he says, "That is the River Sticky.
The only way across is the toll bridge."

All the trucks head toward a narrow,
rickety bridge. One at a time, they roll up
to a gate and put a coin in the slot. The
gate rises, and then they slowly cross.

"It will take years to get through this traffic jam," Hercules grumbles.

"There has to be another way around," Theseus says. "Come on."

The two trucks turn away from the bridge. They race along the banks of the River Sticky.

"It's too far to jump across," Hercules says. "Even for Perseus."

Every ThunderTruck has a special ability. Perseus can jump father than any other truck. Theseus is one of the smartest trucks around. He has an idea.

"Follow me," he beeps.

Up ahead is a steep cliff. The River Sticky flows from a dark tunnel in its rocky wall.

Theseus sees a rusty van stuck in the muck at the edge of the river. He races up to it and uses the rust bucket as a ramp.

Theseus sails into the air. He twists and lands with all four tires on the wall. He races across the cliff and leaps.

When he reaches the other side of the river, he turns to see if Hercules followed him.

THUD!

The mighty ThunderTruck lands next to Theseus.

"Good thinking," Hercules says. "But now the race is back on!" He darts off, leaving Theseus in a cloud of dust.

Theseus speeds after him.

CHAPTER 3

THE MUTT

The ThunderTrucks race along the opposite shore of the River Sticky. Hercules is in the lead. But Theseus is nipping at his mud flaps.

Then the mighty Hercules slams on his brakes. **SCRRREEECH!**

He skids to a stop in front of a narrow tunnel. A stream of dented and rusty trucks enters the tunnel.

Theseus slides up to Hercules. "Why did you stop?" Theseus asks. "We can go around them."

"But I don't think we can get around him," Hercules says.

A truck rolls out of the shadows. It is huge! It looks as if it were built out of the spare parts of other trucks. It blocks their way.

Just then, the black truck rolls up to them. "That is The Mutt," the black truck says in his raspy voice.

"Stop sneaking up on us!" Hercules honks.

"Yeah, who do you think you are?" Theseus asks.

The MonsterTruck does not answer. He just looks ahead.

"The Mutt is your next challenge," he says.

"How do we get past him?" Theseus asks.

"I got this," Hercules rumbles.

Hercules also has a talent. He is the strongest of all ThunderTrucks. He revs his engine **VROOM! VROOM!** as he rolls up to The Mutt.

"Only junkers can pass," The Mutt growls.

"Who's going to stop me!" Hercules rumbles.

The two trucks go bumper to bumper. Hercules revs his engine. **VROOM! VROOM!** He pushes The Mutt back.

Then The Mutt's engine roars. **RRR! RRR!** He shoves Hercules back toward the River Sticky.

Back and forth they push and shove. Their engines roar. **RRR! RRR!** Their tires spin and squeal. A cloud of dust surrounds them.

As they battle, Theseus sees his chance. He sneaks by The Mutt and into the tunnel.

Theseus is almost to the other side of the tunnel when he looks back. Theseus can see that Hercules is exhausted. Puffs of smoke pour out from under his hood, and he has one flat tire. Theseus knows that soon Hercules will bust a piston.

Theseus sneaks up behind The Mutt. He hooks his winch to The Mutt's back bumper. When Hercules revs his engine to give a mighty push, Theseus revs his engine too. **VROOM! VROOM!** He tugs and pulls The Mutt backward. This gives Hercules time to dart around the MonsterTruck.

"Get back here!" The Mutt blares.

But the two ThunderTrucks race

through the other end of the tunnel.

CHAPTER 4

THE JUNKYARD

The MonsterTruck waits for Theseus and Hercules at the other end of the tunnel.

"You are creeping me out!" Hercules honks.

"How did you get past The Mutt?" Theseus asks.

But the strange truck ignores them. Instead, he turns to show the ThunderTrucks what is ahead of them.

The tunnel opens up into a huge cave.

Junky trucks litter its sandy floor.

"This is The Junkyard," the MonsterTruck

says. "Crossing it is your next challenge."

The two ThunderTrucks set off. They

zigzag between trucks. They jump over

dunes. They race bumper to bumper.

"I don't see what is so hard about this,"

Hercules beeps.

But just then, Theseus jerks to a stop.

"Ow!" Theseus beeps. "Something yanked on my back bumper."

Hercules glances back. A rusty tow truck has hooked on to Theseus.

"Hey! Let go of my friend," Hercules blares.

But then he sees something that scares him. All the junked-out trucks are coming to life. Slowly, the wrecks rise and chug their way toward the two ThunderTrucks.

"This isn't good," Theseus beeps. "What will we do?"

"Grab on!" Hercules honks.

Theseus hooks his winch's cable up to Hercules. Then the World's Mightiest ThunderTruck gives a mighty tug. He breaks Theseus free of the rusty tow truck.

"We are surrounded," Theseus beeps.

"Not for long!" Hercules blares.

Hercules darts forward, pulling Theseus along. Then he spins a 360. Theseus sails through the air at the end of the winch's cable.

Hercules holds on to the other end of the cable. His friend flies around in a big circle. As Theseus whips about, he **SMASHES** and **CRASHES** and **BASHES** through the wrecks surrounding them. Then he swings around and lands next to Hercules.

"Whoa!" Theseus says. "That was amazing!"

"But we aren't out of the garage yet," Hercules beeps.

As the pair of ThunderTrucks watch, more and more junkers sputter and chug toward them.

They speed off. But they are still in the middle of The Junkyard and facing hundreds of rust buckets.

"It's Demolition Derby time!" the ThunderTrucks beep.

Hercules crashes into a junker, knocking off its fenders.

Theseus flies over a dune. He lands on a rust bucket and flattens it.

Hercules drives over wreck after wreck, crushing them beneath his tires.

Theseus pinballs from junker to junker, scattering trucks left and right.

The pair **SMASHES** and **CRASHES** and **BASHES** their way through the Underworld.

Spare parts litter the path behind them.

Then they leave The Junkyard behind.

CHAPTER 5

KING OF THE SCRAP HEAP

Hercules and Theseus continue on, but they are no longer racing. Instead, they drive side by side.

"This has been fun," Hercules says.

"Yeah, but we aren't out of the Underworld yet," Theseus says. "Look!"

Up ahead is a huge pile of old trucks. A black truck sits on top of the big heap.

"What are you doing here?" Theseus
asks.

"And where is the exit?"
Hercules asks.

"Don't you want to
know who I am first?" the
MonsterTruck asks.

"Okay, sure," Theseus says.

"As long as you tell us how
to get out of here," Hercules
says.

The truck looks from
Theseus to Hercules. Then
he takes a deep breath.

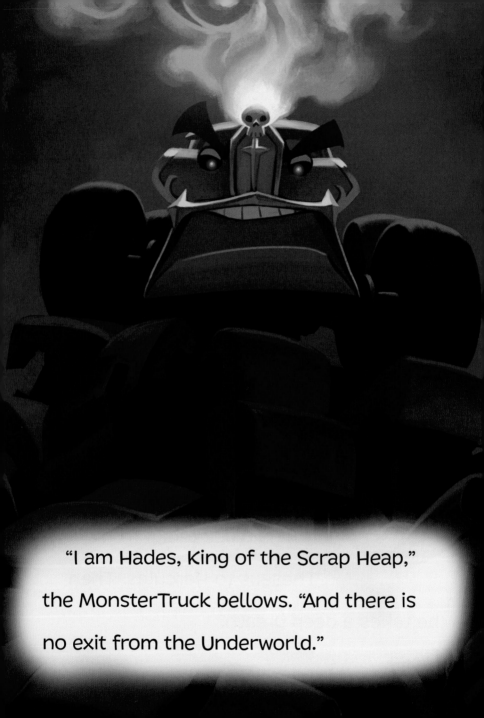

"I am Hades, King of the Scrap Heap," the MonsterTruck bellows. "And there is no exit from the Underworld."

Theseus and Hercules glance at each other.

"Then let's make one!" they shout.

Hercules' engine roars. **RRR! RRR!**

Theseus revs up his engine. **_VROOM!_** **_VROOM._**

Their tires spin and squeal as they take off. They race toward the scrap heap.

"What are you doing?" Hades asks. But the ThunderTrucks don't answer.

When they get to the scrap heap, they race up it.

RRR! RRR! Hercules picks up speed. **_VROOM! VROOM!_** Theseus goes faster and faster.

When they reach the top, they are just a blur.

"Stop!" Hades shouts.

Too late! The ThunderTrucks smash into him. They knock him off the scrap heap. Hades falls and lands with a huge **THUD!**

But Hercules and Theseus do not stop. They use the large pile of junk as a giant ramp. At the top, they fly up into the air. Their speed carries them toward the ceiling of the Underworld.

Then **BOOM!** Together, they crash through the ceiling.

Above, an explosion of dirt and rocks startles a group of ThunderTrucks.

When the dust clears, Theseus and Hercules stand proudly among their friends.

"You're back," Atalanta beeps.

"So who won?" B-phon asks.

"We both did—as a team!" Theseus honks.

"We are the first to escape the Underworld!" Hercules blares.

The other ThunderTrucks congratulate them.

"Come celebrate with us," Perseus says.

"We're heading to the Spare Parts
Buffet for a snack," Odysseus adds.

"I am starving,"
Hercules says.

"Bet I can eat more
oil-covered bolts than
you," Theseus said.

"Can not!"
Hercules rumbles.

"Those two
are like a couple
of spare tires,"
Argonutz says.

"They never change," Atalanta adds.

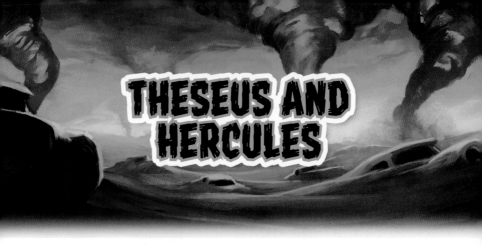

THESEUS AND HERCULES

Underworld Clash was inspired by myths of Theseus and Hercules. Both were famous Greek heroes. Theseus defeated the half-man, half-bull monster known as the Minotaur. Hercules completed 12 incredible feats, from defeating the nine-headed hydra to battling a giant.

During one of his adventures, Theseus traveled to the Underworld. This a place beneath the earth where spirits of the dead go. Hades ruled the Underworld.

Theseus hoped to take Persephone away from her husband Hades. Persephone was goddess of spring.

Hades tricked Theseus. The god asked Theseus to sit and talk. But he had Theseus sit on the Chair of Forgetfulness. Once he sat, Theseus forgot everything. He forgot how to stand. He was trapped!

Luckily for Theseus, one of Hercules' labors was to capture Cerberus. This three-headed dog guarded the gates of the Underworld. While on his quest, Hercules saw Theseus sitting on the Chair of Forgetfulness. Hercules pulled the trapped hero free and then Theseus was able to escape the Underworld. Afterward, Hercules completed his quest and captured Cerberus.

BLAKE HOENA

Blake Hoena grew up in central Wisconsin, where he wrote stories about robots conquering the moon and trolls lumbering around the woods behind his parents' house. He now lives in St. Paul, Minnesota, with his two dogs, Ty and Stich. Blake continues to make up stories about things like space aliens and superheroes, and he has written more than 100 chapter books and graphic novels for children.

FERN CANO

Fernando Cano is an illustrator born in Mexico City, Mexico. He currently resides in Monterrey, Mexico, where he works as a free-lance illustrator and concept artist. He has done illustration work for Marvel, DC Comics, and worked on various video game projects in diverse titles. When he's not making art for comics or books, he enjoys hanging out with friends, singing, rowing, and drawing.

GLOSSARY

competitive (kuhm-PET-i-tiv) - very eager to win, succeed, or excel

decal (DEE-kal) - a picture or label that can be transferred to hard surfaces

dented (DEHN-ted) – to damage something by making a hollow in it

dune (DOON) – a hill or ridge of sand piled up by the wind

repairable (ree-PAIR-uh-buhl) – something broken that can be fixed

traffic jam (TRAF-ik JAHM) – when the movement of vehicles on the road is stopped

Underworld (UHN-dur-wurld) – where the dead go in Greek and Roman mythology

weave (WEEV) – to move from side to side or in and out to get through something

MORE MONSTER MYTHS

ONLY FROM

CAPSTONE